THE CHRISTMAS TREE FAIRY

For Melanie, Inga, Kathrin and Barbara
– with love, Marion

For Keeley and Chloe – *J.C.*

First published in Great Britain in 2005 by Bloomsbury Publishing Plc,
38 Soho Square, London, W1D 3HB

Text copyright © Marion Rose 2005
Illustrations copyright © Jason Cockcroft 2005
The moral rights of the author and illustrator have been asserted

A CIP catalogue record of this book is available from the British Library

ISBN 0 7475 7569 X

Printed in China by South China Printing Co.

10 9 8 7 6 5 4 3 2 1

All papers used by Bloomsbury Publishing are natural, recyclable products made
from wood grown in well-managed forests. The manufacturing processes conform
to the environmental regulations of the country of origin.

THE CHRISTMAS TREE FAIRY

WRITTEN BY

MARION ROSE

ILLUSTRATED BY

JASON COCKCROFT

BLOOMSBURY
CHILDREN'S
BOOKS

M

eredith MacCauley loved her wings.

She wore them everywhere.
She wished one day she could fly,
just like a real fairy.

Then, one dark Christmas night,
Meredith heard a tiny cry.

"Help!"

Meredith tiptoed downstairs.

"Oh!" she gasped.

The Christmas tree fairy had fallen!
She was hanging off a very high
branch.

"I've dropped my wand," the fairy
wailed. "I can't fly without it."

Meredith looked about until she saw
it shining. "It's here," she called.
"Send it back to me," cried the fairy.
"Wave it once and say
'Whizzery Swishery' twice –
that will make it fly!"

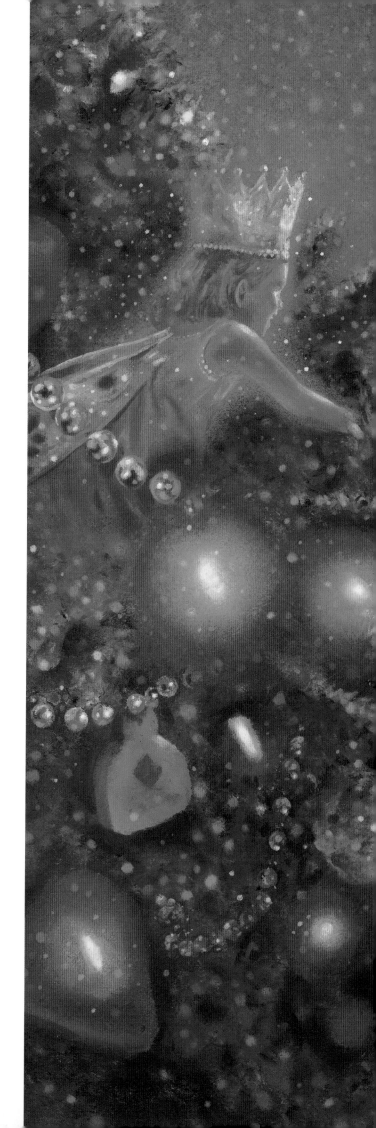

Meredith's heart fluttered like a butterfly. She waved the wand. "Whizzery Swishery! Whishery Swizzery!" she said.

Oh no! Her tongue got in a twist. The spell came out all wrong. Suddenly she was very small and the tree was very TALL.

"Spangle," groaned the fairy. "Whoops! Sorry!" whispered Meredith. "Just bring it up then," the fairy said, a bit bossily. "But hurry!"

Meredith began to climb. It wasn't too hard. The branches made a ladder. And the wand lit the way. But suddenly…

"Is that the star?" asked the shepherd
boy. "I've been waiting ages to see it."
"Er, no," Meredith said. "It's a wand."
"Ooh," the boy sighed. "Where is
that star? I do wish it would come."
Meredith thought.
"I'm going to the Christmas tree
fairy," she said. "I'll tell her your
wish, if you like."
"Oh, will you?" replied the shepherd
boy, gazing at her. "Thank you! Hey,
are you a real fairy?"

But Meredith was already
climbing on . . .

and on . . .

The tree was dark and a bit scratchy. But it smelt nice,
like minty chocolate.
Meredith passed a silver bell and then . . .
"Is that the sleigh?" asked the baby reindeer. "Did I hear it?"
"Er, no," Meredith said. "There's no sleigh yet."

The little reindeer burst into tears. "But why's it taking so long?" she sobbed. "I wish I could meet Santa's reindeer."

Meredith gave the reindeer a hug.

"There, there! I'll tell the Christmas tree fairy. I'm sure she'll help."

"Ooooh!" the reindeer squealed. "You're going to make my wish come true!"

Meredith climbed higher . . .

And higher . . .

Her legs ached but she was getting near the top.

Suddenly . . .

BANG!!!

A strange creature stood in her way. She could smell its fiery breath.
"Ho! Ho! Ho! I am the cracker dragon!" it roared. "If you want to pass you must answer my riddle." It twirled its whiskers fiercely.
Meredith trembled. But she had to go on and help the fairy.
"Ask me then," she said bravely.

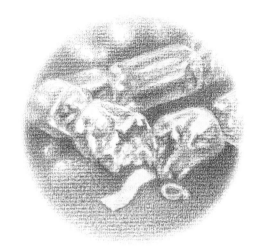

"What light shines most brightly when it is out?" the cracker dragon demanded.

There was a lo-o-ong silence.

Meredith tried to think.

The cracker dragon huffed and puffed while it waited.

"I don't know," Meredith said at last.

"Tell me!"

But the cracker dragon just crumpled into a little heap.

"I can't," he groaned. "I don't know the answer. I lost it ages ago. Oh, how I wish I knew."

He looked so tragic, Meredith patted his claw.

"The Christmas tree fairy will be able to help you, I'm sure," she whispered. "If you could just let me pass."

"Fairies? Wishes? Humbug!" the cracker dragon grumbled. But he moved his claw anyway.

So Meredith MacCauley hurried on.
At last, she reached the high branch.

She crawled all the way out

along it to the fairy.

The fairy beamed at Meredith. She grabbed her wand.
Then she flew ... all around the treetop!
Meredith watched her. The fairy was ... brilliant! If only *she*,
Meredith MacCauley, could do THAT!

The fairy swooped down and sat beside Meredith.
"Now!" she said. "What can I do for you? Three wishes, I expect."
"Gosh!" said Meredith MacCauley.
So these things really did happen!

"Careful what you ask for," the fairy warned. "It's three wishes – no more!"
So Meredith thought very carefully about flying, and all the other fantastic things she could ask for, then she whispered in the fairy's ear.

"Quite sure?" asked the fairy.

Meredith nodded.

"You won't want to change anything?"

Meredith shook her head.

"Well then," said the fairy, and waved her wand.

And Meredith MacCauley's wishes all came true.

"Oh!" breathed the shepherd boy, gazing at the star.

"Look at me!" squeaked the baby reindeer. "She made my wish come true!"

"Ho! Ho! Ho!" the cracker dragon roared again, this time at his own joke: *What light shines most brightly when it is out? A star!*

For a long, magical moment Meredith and the fairy sat together
and watched the night sky.
Then the fairy squeezed Meredith's hand. "Spangle," she said.
"Christmas is nearly here. I shall have to fly you back!"
She raised her wand at once and cried,

"Whizzery Swishery!

Whizzery Swishery!"

And then she, Meredith MacCauley, FLEW!

The next morning, there was another
present under the tree.
Meredith tore it open.
"Ooooh!" she breathed.

Meredith MacCauley loved her new
wings. She wore them everywhere.
And she wished one dark, magical
night she could meet her fairy again.

To Meredith

(And so did all the others!)